DISRUPTIONS

SINGLES 1 - 3

CK PAGE

Cover Design: Teresa Conner | www.wolfsparrowcovers.com

Errands & *Humen* Edited By: Krista Venero - Mountains Wanted Indie Author Services

Infusion Edited By: "Rosie Mundo"

Thank you to Krista Venero & to Rosie for their editing kung fu... *hold up,* you gotta know that all extant errors, mistakes, and issues are solely mine, especially those rare instances where I may have elected to go AEA ("Against Editorial Advice").

Stay Salty.
It's not what you think.
Tea.

Seriously. —"Kenny Mundo"

ERRANDS

SINGLES #1

ERRANDS

A few words of warning... I'm just a guy trying to make ends meet while the whole word is going to shit. I hate errands, and everybody always wants somethin' from all my gettin' things done. Today was no different. A damned grind among a bitch-of-an-ex, her lover, corrupt cops, my double-crossing boss, and friggin' Bruno who's got a thing for beat downs, a bootleg pharmacist pining over a mail order bride, some other local scum-of-the-earth, and just trying to take care of my surviving family—including my late bro's terminally ill daughter. Sometimes a shitstorm is just the company we keep...

.   .   .

√ONE. THE "PHARMACIST" says the drug companies aren't making my niece's medication anymore. Never mind with all the super bugs running wild these days everybody needs it. But hey, not enough profit. What part of thirty-nine billion dollars wasn't "enough"? Only a CEO making three hundred million a year could rationalize math like that. Meanwhile, my niece might die. I look at my watch. On schedule, plenty of time. Still, I hate errands.

√TWO. The tire guy leans on the hood of my truck, relieving himself into a cut-down oil drum. I tell him not to miss and hit my ride. Bart isn't the sharpest tool in the shed, but he's cheap, and, with gas up over nine bucks a gallon, I gotta be picky on maintenance costs. He straightens and drops the siphon into the barrel. He claims the urine helps clean the biodiesel. I think he does it to gross me out. As my ex would say, "the company I keep..."

√THREE. My A/C cuts out right when the clouds clear and the temperature pumps up well over forty degrees Celsius—I know, how un'Merkin of me, but facts are facts. I hate Fahrenheit because it makes no sense—some rich guy made it up and named it after himself—but every degree change in Celsius can be felt on the skin. Damned global warming gone past the tipping point, making everything a shitstorm on a regular basis (oh, the sweet, sweet craptasm brought to you by the First World's "owners," on account of them needin' to be really rich, instead'a just plain old rich. Bastards).

Sweat soaks my shirt and runs down my back almost instantly, despite the breeze through my windows. I wait until the long straightaway, then, steering with my knee, I peel off my shirt and throw it over the bags brimming with crop on the seat beside me.

When I look up, I see the red and blue lights in the mirror.

√FOUR. I stopped earlier at my house and saw my ex with a guy named "Skeeter." It's none of my business. But she kicked me out, citing my scum-of-the-earth associations as some kinda big turn-off, but she fucks a guy named Skeeter? I totally slashed his tires.

.   .   .

√FIVE. My niece lies in the bed, sweating hard, skin pasty, her limbs way too skinny. Only fifteen, her deep brown eyes deserve to take in more of life, not less. My sister-in-law has to work late, so I promise her I'll get the medicine from a "pharmacist" I know. I set the kid up for the next couple of hours with a full water pitcher, a clean hurling bowl, some ice chips, wet rags, some fancy bootlegged electrolyte shit I traded with the "pharmacist" for my own saved up stash last time I was out that way. I tell her I gotta run an errand.

On the way out, I turn over the wedding picture of my dead brother, Jack, and my sister-in-law—wonder why she's been cut out of it. I feel bad about that. My bro was a good guy, dirt poor but a bona fide University graduate and a smarty pants professor too. I loved that guy. That she cut herself out of their wedding picture...it sticks out.

√SIX. The warehouse entry is covered by a shed behind Lenny's hot sister's place. The finest hydroponics this side of the border grows in vaults below ground. No one's around, so I use the key Lenny's hot sister stashed for me—now, I swear I never fooled around with her like she's been telling everybody—and I go below. I gather up what I need for my drop and a little extra...for my niece. I go back for an extra dime for me and hide that one in my truck's chassis. I'm a clever guy.

√SEVEN. Lenny is pissed because I missed the drop. I didn't tell him about the cop, figuring my bloodied nose and split lip says enough. My left eye is swelling shut. I volunteer to make up for it by doing another run for the midnight boat that runs the good shit to college pricks up north. I offer to give up my half of the cut for that run. He accepts, but he has Bruno beat the shit out of me anyway. Lenny's like that.

During the beating, I find out Lenny's "pharmacist" had to move on account of the DEA— most of the damned government's been cut by the Tea Party pricks, but the DEA is a well-funded outfit, go figure. Before my nose gets broken—I guess it got in Bruno's way while he was enjoying himself—I get the cell number of Lenny's "pharmacist" so I can find him. I'm a really clever guy.

√EIGHT. THE "PHARMACIST" takes my niece's last brand name pill and puts it into some kinda gizmo.

"Biggest lie of Big Pharma," he says as he analyzes the contents of the drug. "They claim they charge what they do because the cost of R&D's expensive." He gestures to his modest but efficient lab. The "pharmacist" says anything Big Pharma does for millions in R&D, he can do in an hour for pennies. "Hell, anybody with an 'A' in high school chemistry knows those assholes are full of shit. They just use that R&D money to pad their pockets." He tells me bootleggin' my niece's meds'll take a while. I got another errand anyway.

√NINE. I sneak up behind my house, well, the house I paid for and my ex kept. Through the window I can see them. I don't care about the house, not really, except she's in there fucking Skeeter on my favorite leather sofa. She's not moaning loudly yet, but she's riding him pretty hard... I have about five minutes. I head for his car and retrieve the package he confiscated from me on the sweltering hot straightaway. I slash his tires again, then bust up his windshield for good measure. By the time my ex begins to wail, I'm off for the midnight boat.

·   ·   ·

√TEN. Lenny takes his cut, half of my rightful cut then another third just because he can. I tell him Bruno has better things to do, and we could say I've just paid him an extra third not to beat the shit outta me. Lenny laughs and holds up the little extra bag I took from the warehouse for my niece. I explain, but his sympathy still allows Bruno a few compassionately placed fists to my kidneys and the back of my head.

√ELEVEN. I'm woozy still when the "pharmacist" tells me he can give me a three-month's supply. Only one hitch: he wants me to get him this girl, shows me the mail order catalogue. I have a heart attack when I recognize the picture, then tell him, no problem. I manage a few extra days' supply out of him as a "bonus" when I tell him she's local and I know her.

√TWELVE. I scrape the little stash out of the truck chassis, grateful for my foresight. Said I was clever, right? My broken nose is bleeding again when I go inside my sister-in-law's place. My niece tries to get out of bed to clean my face. The kid's a saint. I hand her the dime and the meds but take care of the broken honker myself.

It's 2:00 a.m. when my sister-in-law gets home. I tell her about the "pharmacist's" offer and the meds. Ever the pragmatist, she takes down his cell number. She feels guilty, about my late bro. I tell her, hey, she deserves a little happiness, that Jack'd be relieved. She seems to feel better. I coulda been a damned fine shrink alright. I promise to pick up some milk in the morning. I'm tired and need to sleep.

√THIRTEEN. Unlucky thirteen. I get milk at the icehouse in front of Lenny's other sister's place and drop it back at my sister-in-law's door. Good thing, because when I go back later to the icehouse for a cold one, Bruno is waiting for me. He's in uniform this time, and so is Skeeter. Shit.

The company I keep...

HUMEN

SINGLES #2

HUMEN

Acertain Hunter watched the herd of antelope thundering across the prairie from the back of the Range Rover. Something had set them on the run, but he couldn't see the back of the herd yet to determine exactly what that something was.

Finally the herd bounded up over the hill he was parked upon, split in two columns racing past him on both sides. He could hear their panicked panting and snorting, wind whistling in their foaming nostrils.

The columns closed together again on the other side of his vehicle and disappeared over the rise into the gully on the other side of the hill. He turned back to the direction they'd come from. For a moment there was nothing.

Then a scrawny, naked man appeared, running raggedly and panting for breath, his maleness swaying exhaustedly. The Hunter dropped his binoculars and stared at the scrawny man, his unkempt beard, his wild dreadlocked hair flecked with bits of prairie grasses, and his naked skin caked with sunbaked muck and grime. The wild man blinked in shock at the Hunter dressed in khaki safari gear atop his white Range Rover, his neatly trimmed handlebar moustache hiding his upper lip.

The two men regarded each other a moment longer.

Then the Hunter spoke, What in the name of bloody Jesus, Martin and Jeffrey are you doing, man?

The wild man blinked and looked around him, confused. He broke into a run around the vehicle following the path of the departed antelope, then he stopped and turned. Could you spare a drop of water, buddy?

The Hunter handed the man his canteen, and the wild man drained it, handing it back while wiping his mouth with the back of a mud-streaked limb.

The Hunter took his emptied canteen, and the

wild man turned and sprinted off with doubled speed. He disappeared over the hill into the gully.

THE HUNTER ENCOUNTERED the wild man again a few days later. The wild man was again chasing antelope, a smaller herd this time. He stopped at the Hunter's vehicle and again asked for water.

This time when he handed the canteen back to the Hunter, the wild man asked if the Hunter wanted to join him.

What are you doing? the Hunter asked, wanting to know first because he was a tactical man, a man of strategy and cunning.

I'm chasing antelope, the wild man replied.

I can see that, the Hunter countered. Why?

The wild man blinked, confused. Why not?

The Hunter screwed his face up, and he leaned on his gun. What do you mean, why not?

The wild man glanced over his shoulder at the herd. The antelope had stopped at the top of the next rise as if waiting for the wild man to continue his pursuit. They cropped at the prairie grasses and flicked their stubby tails in the air.

The wild man turned back to the Hunter and explained, I'm going to catch one.

Ah! the Hunter responded. You are a Hunter like me!

The wild man looked at the man's gun, the Hunter stroking the stock with a smooth hand.

The wild man shook his head. Nah, I just want to catch one...you know, give it a hug.

The Hunter was flabbergasted. A hug?! Well, Jesus and Moses ganging up on Margaret, man, why on earth for?

The wild man smiled and stretched his scrawny limbs. I want to know if it can be done, he said, his broken broad teeth catching the sunlight.

The Hunter blinked, his turn to be confused.

The wild man invited, You wanna come try too?

Try to what?

You know, catch an antelope. Give it a hug; see if it can be done?

The Hunter blinked back for such a long time without saying anything, the wild man gave up. Well, if you change your mind, I'll be out there. The wild man pointed to the open plains.

He ran off.

THE HUNTER ENCOUNTERED the wild man chasing herds of antelope of varying sizes a dozen more times over the next week. Finally, one morning, as a herd broke through his camp, scattering his gear and trampling his rifle to bits, the Hunter accepted the wild man's hand, helping him onto his feet.

The wild man grinned stupidly and waved at the herd that had stopped a few dozen meters in the distance.

So, what do you say, Hunter, ole friend? Wanna try it yet?

The Hunter looked at his ruined camp, his shattered rifle and the herd. His left eye narrowed, and he rubbed his moustache smooth. Alright, then, how is this done?

The wild man clapped the Hunter on the back proudly. You won't regret this, Huntery-Pal. It's exhilarating indeed. Come on!

He broke off into a run, and the Hunter followed, shedding his khaki safari jacket and wisely grabbing his canteen.

The Hunter had to stop quite often as they ran in pursuit of the antelope herd across the prairie. Several times, the Hunter lost sight of the wild man and was left to look around, fearing he was hopelessly lost. But then, after a while, the herd would pass by heading in the opposite direction, followed closer and closer behind by the wild man.

The Hunter had to eventually shed his shirt, then his boots as the heat became unbearable in the afternoon. At nightfall, he rubbed his raggedy feet as the wild man made camp simply by sprawling in the coarse grass near the herd he'd been chasing most of that day. The Hunter did the same, exhausted and hungry.

After a morning meal of prairie grass roots and seeds, the duo set out again after another herd of antelope.

The Hunter soon forgot about his camp, his rifle, even his canteen, and along the way, his clothes. They ranged farther and farther from his vehicle, but he was caught up and consumed by the thrill of the chase. The feel of the ground pounding under his feet, the rippling sensation of his muscles burning in the sunlight, the grasses whispering past his now-bared thighs—he had tossed off his pants three days into the antelope chasing. It took a week longer before he eschewed his boxer shorts running *au naturel* like the wild man. The swinging of his manhood was a bit uncomfortable at first, but after a few days, his body adjusted to the rhythm of running all day long, and he didn't seem to notice at all.

The men eventually stopped talking, communicating in gestures and whistles, mimicking their prey. They were getting faster too, closing what was initially up to a fifty-meter gap to a bare five, and then three. The Hunter's natural skills for strategy and tactics were energized, enlarged, even, and the two wild men began to employ flanking maneuvers and quick turns, using the terrain to slow the antelope and force them to stay in gullies while the feral human pursuers flew across the ridgetops on either side.

The Hunter came to appreciate his wild brother. He respected the man's endurance and capacity for skill and agile tactics on the chase. He even came to admire the wild, flailing dreadlocks and lean limbs. The Hunter's own hair soon grew long and dreadlocked like his mentor's, his moustache trailing down past his mouth and chin into a willowy beard flying in the wind as he ran, and ran, and ran.

DAYS PASSED INTO WEEKS, and weeks engorged into months. The weather began to change and grew colder at night. The afternoons were still hot and sultry, but the men had acclimatized to the plain now, their mud-caked bodies growing lean and taut.

Then one day, it happened.

The two feral hu-men had successfully cornered a small herd of young antelope in a low gully. They flanked the herd, and soon both were running apace of the wild-eyed animals.

The wild man glanced over at the Hunter, and he back, exchanging the signal they'd worked out over many months of chasing antelope, the signal for the catch. The wild man let out a yelp of glee as he hurdled his left leg over the back of a young doe, landing in the middle of the fleeing herd. The Hunter did the same with his right leg, pinning two antelope between their sprinting bodies.

Suddenly arms flung wide open and closed, clutching the frightened four-leggeds around their necks. The antelope-feral human hug lasted for a second—a second that enlarged into a minor eternity until it erupted in ebullient, overwhelming joy, then was broken as both creatures became aware of their heightened discomfort the strange humen behavior had struck in their antelopian minds. With viscous snorts of exasperation, the four-legged pair bucked into the air, out of the arms of the two naked men.

Arms and legs, beards and dreadlocks, male members and knees tumbled together in a giddy sprawl, lurching to a skidding halt across the bent grasses.

The two wild men looked up into the feral blue sky above them, their chests heaving as they caught their breath. They looked at each other and high-fived their success, laughing hysterically in triumph and elated exhaustion.

As the sun sank lower toward the western horizon, the men finally sat upright. They looked at each other and smiled broadly again. Then, hands clasped together, brothers in success, the feral men rose from the prairie grass and faced the rising moon in the east.

We did it, the wild man breathed.

We caught an antelope, the Hunter finished. And we gave 'em a hug.

They looked at each other and embraced.

It can be done, one said.

Indeed, it can be done, said the other.

Arms over the others' shoulders, the two men headed in the direction of a gully they knew had a pond. They had earned a long moonlight swim and a drink and a bath.

Whom shall we run down next?

I dunno.

Wonder if a gazelle is any faster than an antelope?

I saw some up north a few days back...

INFUSION

SINGLES #3

INFUSION

Her hand drifted across the back of his shoulders as she passed behind him. He didn't look up but smiled as he contemplated his freshly infused tea. The tea rested in his favorite Japanese potted cup, carefully crafted by his college roommate's father in a mountain village whose name was known only to a few of its inhabitants, the rest barely cared to know. He could feel the soul of its maker infusing the tea with peaceful karma, the good will mingling with the hot tea, concentric rings spreading outward from the energy center of the cup. He liked tea. He loved the cup. He loved contemplating his tea.

Her fingers reluctantly left his forearm having trailed all the way down his limb, as she found her seat. She pulled the paper to her across the hand-hewn table's surface. Her movement was always the same and on one level it annoyed him tremendously on another level he was ambivalent and on another level—his revelations always came in threes—he liked how she moved. But that in itself could piss him off too.

"This parade thing is such a farce."

He didn't reply, her words interrupting the flow of the aroma rising from the cup to his nostrils. He savored what he could from the rising fragrance before her next comment demanded his participation.

"Don't you think?"

"No. I don't think."

"About what?"

"The parade, it's a pageant," he corrected her.

She curled her lip and trained her piercing amber-green eyes on his teacup.

"What's the difference?" She replied slowly. "A pageant has a parade, all in the same event."

He sipped the tea and felt the warm botanical bouquet rolling into his mouth, languid and tumbling with a pleasurable sensation. In the leaves he could see the floral young women, the finest of the city, arrayed for the pleasure and titillation of the old men and elites of the region.

"What counts are the origins of the damned thing," he said, not looking up.

"Oh not this again," she complained.

She put up her hands, mockingly adding in sing-song, "Don't tell me, it's a pagan thing or some such?"

"Of course. Most things genuinely are."

She rolled her eyes and picked up her tea again, her lips moving to sip from the cup as she intoned. "Enlighten me, oh wise one."

Unfazed, he continued, "Ancient rituals, fertility, midwinter, boredom, ways to spread the genetic assets of a village."

He half closed his eyes, inhaling the rising bouquet from the cup, the moment fading fast, pushed away by her words, which he loved, truly, but also felt chafing his moment.

"Everything with you is sex."

"Of course it is," he replied matter of factly.

"Puh-leez."

"It's true..

He set the cup down precisely, the entire circle of pottery resting on the table surface all at the same time. "The town fathers gather all the young hotties and put them on display, then later on after the parade, the hordes have their ways with them in some debauching rite which defeats boredom, spreads genetic material around and helps maintain the local patriarchy's choke-hold on power."

"You're so demented.. She shuddered, disgusted.

"No, just informed.. He peered at his tea then raised his eyes to the steam curling above it. "It's the same now as then, only now the debauching takes place in the minds of the town fathers instead of out in the open. It was honest then and now it's dishonest."

"Nobody but you would have such perverted daydreams from a simple parade. What about the historical significance of it?"

He turned his cup slowly.

"But that *is* the historical significance of it. The powerful control the serfs through demeaning public display and then call it a pageant, to make it all nice and pretty."

"I suppose this is somehow connected to a conservative plot too?. She said with a noisy fluff of the paper, turning it to page six without looking at the words.

"It usually is."

"Why do you do that?"

"What?"

"Why do you link sexual nonsense, where there clearly isn't anything sexual, with conservative patriarchal plots to maintain control of the masses?"

He shrugged, disappointed that his tea moment had long passed.

"Because it's true."

"No it's not," she countered.

"Explain it another way then."

She put the paper down and looked out the window.

A finch was hopping on the snow-covered branch outside the window, searching in its jerking, tilting way for seeds left behind by the squirrels.

"Sometimes people just like to have fun, feel attractive, be out in public with each other, have a parade, god forbid."

"That explains what happens but not why it happens," he challenged.

"There is no 'why', just what happens. Most people aren't that deep."

"Therein lies the source of the autocrat's power."

"No, just how people behave in communities."

"No, how autocrats control communities to prop themselves up so they don't have to do any work themselves. Then they cover it up by propaganda which the oppressed people buy into because of their delusional uninformed optimism, which is really just a subconscious way of enabling the dysfunctional elites to maintain the perverse order of things."

"Your world is cruel and perverted."

"Maybe it wouldn't be so perverted if I had a reason to not think about sex..

Silence.

"You're such a prick."

"How would you know, you haven't tried being around it in god-knows-how-long."

She reached over and collected his teacup, then took a sip.

"It's cold," she said, making a face trying to change the subject.

"Cold is my life."

"We did it last month. You want it twenty times a goddamned day. No woman could keep up with that."

"Good god almighty, last month, and how long before the next time, a year?"

Silence.

"Most committed partners do things from a love for each other. Love means affection. I never signed on to be a eunuch."

"You're not a eunuch."

"I'm not?"

"No, eunuchs are not loved by women. You are, god knows why."

"Show me where they're hiding, these women who love me."

"You just want too much, that's all."

She picked up the cup and moved away from the table, headed for the microwave.

"Don't put that into that damned contraption!"

She stopped, placing the cup inside and closing the door.

"Why not?" She said as she punched in the buttons and hit "Start."

"For fuck's sake, woman!" He pleaded. "You'll ruin the infusion of the subtle and varied essences with that low-grade radiation."

She grinned sadistically. She loved the look of horror on his face. Served him right for treating her like dirt because of her stunted libido—a problem surely caused by the stress of having to live with such a man.

"It's cold and this will heat it up. The radiation is minor and won't hurt you."

"Not me, the tea... it'll wreck the tea."

"It'll take you twenty minutes to heat up the tea over that charcoal boiler thingy of yours..."

"Twenty minutes will allow the essences to gently become excited..."

"Excited, isn't that a conservative perversion?" She mocked.

His face reddened then he exhaled in surrender.

"Conservatives don't drink tea, they drink that latte shit or mocha frappasuction, or whatever it is. As long as it's sold in a franchised cookie cutter poison box, in a overly bleached paper cup mined from the clear cut forests of yesteryear..."

"... 'And for a dozen dollars, a little less than what it really costs the environment,' yeah, I know the drill."

She sighed and stopped the microwave.

He watched her pull the teapot back over to the broiler and stoke up the flame. She put a new cup with new leaves into a fresh bag and perched it into the cup, suspended by the bamboo skewer from the rim of the cup.

"I'll make you a new cup."

He softened a little.

"Thank you. Nice of you to be so merciful."

"You should appreciate my mercy more often."

He was still eyeing the ruined cup of steaming tea.

"You should drink the one you ruined."

"No problem."

She rolled her eyes as she said it and then picked up the steaming cup and brought it back to the table.

She sat drinking the "ruined" tea while he folded his hands precisely and slowly circled one fingertip around the opposite fingertip. His ears were attuned to the sound of the filtered water roiling in the teapot behind him.

The silence between them snapped at them both like a rabid dog.

He got up after a moment and went to the broiler. The teapot thermometer read 82.2°C and he pulled it off the flame. He opened the lid of the teapot and dipped the bamboo ladle into the steaming water. He turned the cup precisely, the bag tilted just so, hanging beneath the skewer. Then he poured the water carefully into the cup. There was a flash of steam as the finely ground leaves swelled and rapidly expanded, the water infusing the tea and releasing the essential oils and botanical essences into the cup.

He prepared a second cup and bag and repeated the ritual. He pulled out a small tray and placed each cup upon it. He turned with tray in hand. He offered the first cup to her, a peace offering, a truce requested.

She finished her cup and set it aside as he placed the tray on the table between them. She watched as he handled the cup with a delicate touch and placed the cup before her. He turned it so the emblem etched into the rim faced her and then moved it a few centimeters forward towards her.

She put her hand on the new cup and waited as he sat down before she repeated the same for him. They drank for a moment in silence.

He put his cup down precisely and inhaled slowly.

"So, you wanna have sex?"

She blinked slowly at him then shook her head.

"Ugh, you're an ass..."

She sat back in her chair.

"Maybe next week."

"Let me guess, if I behave myself?"

She smirked.

BEFORE YOU GO...

Go right now to pageturn.com and subscribe to my official reader list so you won't miss good stuff: bonus stories & discover my author-buds you will definitely want to read.

Can't get enough? Like my author page on Facebook, follow me on Twitter and Instagram. I try to keep things irreverent and funny... ya know, before the Apocalypse messes everything up.

If you enjoyed *Disruptions*, please write a rave review at Amazon and Goodreads. Reviews help other readers & positive gushin' shares the love. Think of it as helpin' a dude survive every time you share and spread the word.

Your positive comments and reviews are greatly appreciated. —C.K.

ALSO BY CK PAGE

Novellas and Short Stories

This'n Apocalypse Or Not? *-a post-apocalypse/liminal novella*

Drive-Up *-a sentimental, fabulist/sci-fi short*

Is Blood Thicker *-a liminal fiction short*

From Singles, a monthly short literary fiction series:

Disruptions *-a trio of Singles short-short stories 1-3*

Errands *-a short-short literary fiction story #1*

Humen *-a short-short literary fiction story #2*

Infusion *-a short-short literary fiction story #3*

Novels

Love, Death, & The After, a post-apocalypse/sci-fi series:

Love, Death & The After: Darkness Book 1

Love, Death & The After: Abandoned Spaces Book 2

Love, Death & The After: Never Again Book 3

From the Costeros Saga, a post-apocalypse/sci-fi collection of tales and novels:

Costera: Pacific's Daughter *-curated novel*

Costeros: Echo *-novella*

Steamy Romance:

Penumbra *-a contemporary novel and modern fable*

ABOUT THE AUTHOR

 **Christopher "CK" Page** wrangled a Creative Writing degree from an unsuspecting Californian university and authored & published numerous speculative fiction stories and a few novels, among other shenanigans. Christopher writes from overpopulated, under-watered California with a brilliant Mate and some Beasts (all knuckleheads of *felus domesticus*)—there are some grown-up Offspring somewhere—"Call yer father!" Sexy as hell, he stays fit in retirement from a career as a referee with US Soccer, CIF/NFHS, and US Lacrosse.

For more books and updates:
www.pageturn.com

Made in the USA
Monee, IL
19 August 2020